A Shocking Discovery

With her gloved finger, Agent Scully pried open one of Jack Hammond's eyelids. She looked at the dead eye beneath. The lens had fused into a cloudy membrane, hiding the pupil. She checked the other eye.

"There are cataracts over both eyes," she said. She looked over at Mulder. "Probably heat-induced."

"Probably?" Fox Mulder looked at his partner with mild astonishment.

Mulder turned and picked up the plastic bag on the anatomical scale next to him. Inside the bag was a charred piece of flesh, burned almost—but not quite—past the point of recognition.

It was a human heart.

"*Probably* heat-induced?" Mulder asked again. "The kid's heart was cooked inside his chest."

THE (X) FILES™

VOLTAGE

a novel by Easton Royce

based on the television series
The X-Files created by Chris Carter
based on the teleplay
written by Howard Gordon

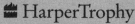 HarperTrophy
A Division of HarperCollinsPublishers

VOLTAGE

Chapter ONE

The parking lot of the strip mall had a wet, oily sheen. With one storm gone and another one on its way, few people were out. Besides, the tiny town of Connerville, Oklahoma, just about shut down at eight P.M., and it was already eleven.

The strip mall itself was an unimpressive place—a laundry, a convenience store, and a video arcade. The convenience store was inconveniently closed, as was the laundry. But the video arcade never shut down before midnight.

Tonight there was only one car in the lot. It was a classic convertible with its top down—as if it dared the sky to rain.

That was the kind of guy its owner was. Jack Hammond had a chip on his shoulder the size of Mount Rushmore. And now, after a miserable night of delivering pizza, he took out his anger on the games in the arcade.

Since he was the only customer, he figured no one would distract him as he played Virtual Massacre II. He imagined himself as the virtual fighter on the screen, aiming roundhouse kicks at his opponent. It wasn't as big a thrill as playing high-school football, but Jack's football days had ended about two years and twenty pounds earlier.

Jack hit the buttons and tugged at the joystick like a gearshift. It had been months since he'd gotten his initials on the high score list. Some loser named D.P.O. had every high score locked up. Jack hoped he might squeeze his way onto the list today—but he had already lost two lives.

And was about to lose a third.

"Uh . . . hey," said a dull voice behind him. "I was playing that."

Jack took a quick glance over his shoulder. A mealy-looking kid in a greasy baseball cap and a T-shirt was standing behind him.

"I just went to the bathroom," said the kid. "Now I'm back."

The kid looked like a loser. Jack guessed he was about nineteen, and by the look of him that wasn't just his age, but his IQ as well. He had the kind of in-bred face that Jack couldn't stand. Kids like that gave small towns a bad name.

Jack returned his attention to the game, but it was too late. He was just in time to watch as his virtual fighter's neck was snapped by a lethal karate chop.

"Even good guys blow it," said a throaty, synthe-

sized voice from the screen. The voiced laughed as GAME OVER, bright and red, blinked in Jack Hammond's face.

Jack slammed the side of the machine and turned to the scrawny kid who had blown his game. "You got a problem?" he growled.

The kid wouldn't look up at him. He just kept his eyes in the shadow of his baseball cap.

"It's my game. I was playing here."

"Were you, pinhead? Well, now you're not." Jack dug in his pocket and slapped a few quarters down on the game, claiming his territory.

The kid offered a sorry little grin. "Maybe you didn't hear me right," he said. "It's my game."

"It's his game," echoed another voice.

Jack turned to see a fat kid with straggly, long hair and a coin changer on his belt. His name was Bart, but everyone called him Zero, for obvious reasons.

"And what are you, the game police?"

"No, I'm the night manager," said Zero proudly, "and I'd step away if I were you."

It started to dawn on Jack that maybe this scrawny kid was, in fact, the mysterious D.P.O. "Okay," Jack said. "You want to play a game? We'll play a game." But a video match wasn't what he had in mind.

He reached out and grabbed the scrawny kid by

his dirty T-shirt, lifting him an inch or two off the floor.

"I go first," Jack said. He threw the kid against the game. The kid's baseball cap fell off as he went down, revealing a huge scar across the side of his head. "What'd ya do? Get your brain removed, or something?"

After that, Jack figured the kid would just slink away—crawl back under whatever rock he had come from. But he didn't crawl away.

That was when the power went out.

"Oh, man," said Zero, "you really shouldn't have done that."

Still on the ground, Darin Oswald took a deep, slow breath. He didn't do it to calm his anger, but to force it to build. The arcade was dark now, lit only by the dim vapor lamp that buzzed over the parking lot.

Darin picked up his baseball cap and stood up. Calmly he put the cap back on his head. Even with his fury building he kept his cool. It would be more fun that way.

The jukebox in the corner suddenly came on all by itself. Clearly, this was not your ordinary power outage. A song by Darin's favorite band, The Nightwalkers, played loud and rude.

Darin stepped up to Jack Hammond. He remembered the big jock from high school—although they'd traveled in very different circles.

"So is it my turn now?" Darin asked. The quiet in his voice was eerie, like the calm before a storm.

Hammond backed off. There was a hint of fear in his face. "I'm not wasting my time," he snarled, and stalked toward the exit.

The open air of the parking lot was a welcome relief. Jack wasn't sure what had just happened back there in the video arcade, and he really didn't feel like finding out.

He hopped into his convertible and turned the key in the ignition. Suddenly the radio came on—loud. The song sounded familiar—way too familiar.

It was the same song that had been playing on the jukebox back in the arcade. Something by The Nightwalkers.

Coincidence, that's all, thought Jack. Still, he fumbled with the knob when he turned the radio off. But the song continued to play.

It was impossible. He spun the tuner through a dozen different stations.

The song still played.

And there, in the door of the arcade, stood the scrawny scar-headed kid, calmly staring out at him.

5

Hammond threw the car into first gear and floored the accelerator. The tires spun on the wet pavement, and he fishtailed across the parking lot.

There were some weird things going on in this town. First there had been the scientists up the hill with their lightning rods. Then there'd been the strange string of freak accidents down at the crossroads. But nothing could be weirder than that kid in the arcade. The more distance Jack could put between them, the better.

His car was about to escape the parking lot when the engine died. It didn't stall. It didn't sputter. It just died, and the car rolled to a stop.

Jack frantically turned the key in the ignition. Nothing.

Yet the radio still blared.

And the creepy kid was in the doorway of the arcade, silently watching.

There was a burst of light followed by a sharp *crack*. Jack spun to see the pizza delivery sign on his antenna burst into flames. It was the only warning he got. Suddenly a shock seemed to explode from the center of his chest, out to his legs, arms, and head. He could feel his eyes bulging, his body convulsing violently, bouncing in the seat. The pain in his muscles was unbearable.

All at once, Jack Hammond knew he wasn't getting out of that parking lot alive.

His fingers knotted with the voltage flying through them. He reached out to try to open the door, but he was shaking so violently that his head smashed the side door. There was nothing he could do . . . nothing but feel himself die.

From the doorway of the arcade, Darin Oswald watched without a bit of emotion as Jack Hammond died.

At last Darin released his hold on the car radio. The parking lot fell silent. A wisp of smoke drifted up from the front seat of the convertible toward the streetlamp.

Darin turned and headed back into the arcade, where Zero dutifully waited for him. Smiling, Zero offered him a quarter—but Darin didn't need it.

Wiping a trace of sweat from his brow, Darin stood before Virtual Massacre II. The machine switched on—like magic.

He twitched a muscle in his face, and a new game began, just as if he had dropped in a quarter.

"I feel a new record coming on, man," Darin said as he moved forward and took the controls.

Chapter TWO

Like so much else in Connerville, the Wharton County Building was unremarkable, colorless, and old. Most people passing by never gave it a second thought. After all, what was there? The county tax assessor, social services, the hall of records. And, of course, the county coroner.

Stan Buxton had seen quite a lot as county coroner—but nothing that had ever brought out the FBI before. He watched nervously as the young, female FBI agent examined the boy whom Buxton had pronounced dead the night before.

She and her intense-looking partner had arrived only thirty minutes earlier. They'd waltzed into his office waving their IDs, proclaiming they were there as part of a federal investigation. Then the young lady had informed Stan, as smartly as you please, that she was a trained pathologist. She insisted on examining the Hammond boy's remains—immediately.

Buxton wasn't used to having his work second-guessed. He worried that this woman from Washington, D.C., might find something he had missed. Especially since the cause of death, as he had determined it, could be considered odd: The boy had been struck and killed by lightning, out of a clear night sky.

Just like the others . . .

The woman leaned over the body, peering professionally through her protective goggles into the dead boy's ear canal. Then she rotated the corpse's head ninety degrees and peered into the other ear. Finally she straightened up and looked at her partner.

"Both eardrums are ruptured," Agent Dana Scully said. Her voice was flat—with only, perhaps, the slightest trace of a sigh.

Scully was used to examining dead bodies, many in far worse condition than this one. But she could never completely push from her mind the awareness that this mass of flesh and bone before her had once been a living human being—a real person, filled with hopes, ambitions, dreams.

Her gloved finger pried open one of Jack Hammond's eyelids. She looked at the dead eye beneath. The lens had fused into a cloudy white membrane, hiding the pupil. She checked the other eye.

"There are cataracts over both eyes," she said, her voice still neutral. She looked over at Mulder again. "Probably heat-induced."

"Probably?" Fox Mulder responded, looking at his partner with mild astonishment.

Mulder turned and picked up the plastic bag on the anatomical scale next to him. He held it out for Scully, as if to remind her how strange this case already was. Inside the bag was a charred piece of flesh, burned almost—but not quite—past the point of recognition.

It was a human heart.

"The kid's heart was cooked right inside his chest," Mulder said to Scully, in the "explain this" sort of tone he often used with his partner.

"I have to admit," the coroner began grudgingly, "I've never seen that kind of localized tissue damage, but—"

"This charring along the sternum," Scully said to Mulder, cutting Buxton off, "these rib fractures—they're consistent with electrocution or exposure to high-voltage direct current." She pointed inside the hole in the dead boy's chest.

Buxton nodded, but Scully just kept looking at her partner. Mulder met her gaze, challenging her—*daring* her—to go on with her explanation.

"But I see no point of contact," she said, turning to Buxton for confirmation.

And that's the problem, she thought. The one simple fact that made an easy explanation impossible.

It was as if the kid had been cooked from the inside out—as though he'd been placed inside a giant microwave oven.

"Best I can figure," Buxton said, choosing his words with care, "is that the lightning struck the car and killed the kid on contact."

That doesn't makes any sense, Scully thought. She wondered if Buxton knew that. And she wondered if she'd be able to do any better when the time came for her to give her own opinion.

Scully looked back at Mulder and considered him carefully. She knew all too well the way his mind worked. She wondered if he was already thinking *cover-up.*

Of course, since she'd become Mulder's partner, she had seen for herself things she had never dreamed could exist in a world she'd thought she understood. Parasitic worms frozen in arctic ice . . . a human monster who digested other people's fat . . .

The coroner's gaze shifted to the door behind her. Scully followed his eyes to a large, imposing presence now filling the doorway.

Sheriff John Teller.

Scully and Mulder generally made every effort to cooperate with local law enforcement when they were assigned to a case. When they had arrived in Connerville, however, Sheriff Teller had been out on a call, so they had come straight to the coroner's office. It was a simple oversight in protocol, but one that Scully suddenly knew would haunt them.

She turned back to the coroner. "Did you find contact wounds on any of the other five victims?" she asked him.

Buxton rocked back on his heels slightly, apparently more confident now that the sheriff was there to back him up.

"I'd have to look back at my notes," he said brusquely, brushing the question aside. He paused, then forged ahead. "Look, it's pretty clear to me what killed all these kids."

Mulder was staring down at the body on the table. "Lightning," he said, with a sarcasm only Scully caught.

"Well, yeah," the coroner agreed.

In the doorway the sheriff crossed his arms and cleared his throat. Scully knew the examination was over. She took off the protective goggles and looked at the coroner. She couldn't let this go without a fight.

"Are you aware that only about sixty people die from lightning strikes across the country each year?" she asked. "And five of those happened right here in Connerville?"

"I know it's statistically improbable," the coroner replied, "but—"

"There were only *four* deaths." It was Sheriff Teller who interrupted. He strode powerfully into the room and clapped a reassuring hand on the coroner's shoulder. "It's okay, Stan. You don't have to defend your work."

The coroner nodded his thanks.

Teller continued softly, "Give me a minute with our new 'friends' here from the FBI, okay?"

"Yeah, sure," Buxton muttered. "I'll be in my office."

Sheriff Teller turned his attention to the two FBI agents. "In case you didn't know, I'm the sheriff around here. I just got word there was an FBI investigation."

Mulder and Scully exchanged glances. *We should have stuck to protocol,* Scully thought. She flashed Teller her warmest smile.

"I'm Agent Scully—" she began.

"I know who you are," Teller shot back. "I just want to know what you think you're doing here."

The smile faded from Scully's face. She glanced back at Mulder for support—but he had stepped away. He was now studying, with intense interest, the sheet covering Jack Hammond's body.

13

"These deaths," Scully explained to the sheriff, "match other local cases of multiple fatalities attributed to lightning, with the same . . . inconclusive evidence."

"Inconclusive to whom?" Teller snorted. He put his hands in his pockets and cocked his head. His voice suddenly took on a folksy, condescending tone. "Do you know anything about lightning, *Mizz* Scully?"

"Yes."

"Did you know lightning kills several people a year at home, in their showers or talking on the phone? That people have seen it dancing on the ground in balls?" Teller was on a roll now. "But scientists—even the best scientists—don't really know what makes lightning work."

"I didn't know that," Scully said. She glanced at Mulder again for help, but he offered none.

Sheriff Teller smiled. "Well, I know that, because I have breakfast with those scientists every morning down at the local diner."

Scully blinked. "I don't understand."

"That's as clear as glass." Teller stopped talking long enough to smirk. "Do you know what we manufacture here in Connerville? What one of our little local commodities is?"

Scully said nothing.

"We make lightning," Teller said. "Down at the Astadourian Lightning Observatory out on Route Four. One hundred ionized rods pointing at the sky, designed to stimulate lightning."

Scully sighed. "I didn't know that, either," she admitted.

"That's because you didn't do your homework, did you?" the sheriff said scornfully. "You came here to do work that's already been done."

There was something in the sheriff's attitude, something in his certainty, that annoyed Scully. He reminded her of someone, but she couldn't quite pin down who.

"With all due respect, sir," she said finally, "these autopsies don't add up."

"Based on what?"

"Based on my opinion as a medical doctor."

This stopped Teller for a moment, and he allowed himself a small smile. "Then based on your medical opinion," he asked dryly, "what do you think this boy died of?"

Scully opened her mouth to answer, then closed it. She glanced one more time at Mulder. Still no help there. Finally she looked back at Teller. "Well . . . since there's no other explanation right now, I'd have to agree that the most probable cause of death . . . is lightning."

Teller looked at her, flicked his eyes toward Mulder, then nodded, satisfied. "And I won't have you, or anyone else, suggesting otherwise to this boy's family."

The sheriff paused meaningfully, to make sure his words had registered; then he turned on his heel and strode from the room.

Scully continued looking at the space the sheriff had filled. "Feel free to jump in anytime," she murmured to her silent partner.

"Why?" Mulder said at last, smiling as he walked to her side. "You were doing just fine."

Scully sighed. It was not shaping up to be a good day. First the sheriff's attitude had put her off. Then, even worse, she had ended up agreeing with him.

"Do you have a theory about what's happening here?" she asked.

"I just don't think it's lightning."

"Then what do you think it is? What do you think we'll find?" Scully knew she could be treading on dangerous ground with that question.

Mulder considered. "Well, I'd sure like to know who's funding their little lightning factory . . ." He paused, and Scully could almost see his mind racing through the possibilities. "Tell me the truth,

16

Scully. Do *you* think that kid was hit by lightning?"

Scully hated moments like this, when Mulder asked her to make a judgment before all the evidence was in.

"Just because an autopsy's results don't give you a cut-and-dried answer doesn't mean they're wrong," she insisted.

Mulder pressed. "So Teller's explanation works for you?"

Scully felt torn. "The only possible *scientific* conclusion is that Jack Hammond was killed by lightning." Maybe if she could convince Mulder, she could convince herself.

But Mulder was far from convinced.

"Well, this local lightning is even more predictable than Teller realizes. It seems to have a definite preference for the type of person it strikes."

"What are you talking about?" Scully asked.

Like a magician pulling a rabbit from his hat, Mulder opened the case file and pulled out a piece of paper. He presented it to Scully.

"Look. They're all male, all between the ages of seventeen and twenty-one." He glanced up at Scully. "Just like Jack Hammond."

Scully considered this new fact. The coroner had said the number of Connerville lightning victims was statistically improbable. This new information drove the statistics toward the realm of the impossible.

"Let's see where Jack Hammond was killed," Mulder suggested. "Maybe we'll find something we can agree on."

Chapter THREE

Jack Hammond's car had not yet been towed away from the strip mall. Pending further investigation, the sheriff's department had set orange cones around the vehicle.

Fox Mulder crouched behind the car, looking at the skid marks on the parking lot blacktop.

Behind him, Scully was looking inside the car.

"The police found Hammond in his car at seventeen minutes past midnight," she said, reading from the file. "The entire electrical system was shorted out. All the circuitry and wiring had melted."

She walked over to Mulder, who was still crouching, contemplating the meaning of the skid marks. He pointed them out to Scully.

"Looks like he was trying to get away in a big hurry."

Scully looked at the marks. "Get away from what?"

Mulder stood up and scanned the stores in the strip mall. "When was Jack Hammond's last pizza delivery?"

Scully checked the file. "Sometime between eleven and eleven thirty. Why?"

"All these stores would have been closed by eleven." His eyes stopped on the video arcade. "Except maybe that one."

Mulder and Scully paused for a moment to allow their eyes to adjust to the dim, blue-tinged light in the arcade. At the front counter a husky teen was slowly counting quarters into paper tubes.

"Ten . . . eleven . . . uh . . . twelve . . ." He was leaning over the counter, giving each coin his full attention. "Thirteen . . ."

"Excuse me," Scully said to the top of his head.

The teen held up a dirty finger and continued counting. "Um . . . fourteen . . ."

Scully and Mulder exchanged wry glances. Impatient as always, Mulder wandered off to explore the deeper recesses of the video arcade.

Scully turned back to the clerk in front of her and tried again.

"Excuse me, please," she said, more insistently this time.

A sweaty, pimple-pocked face glanced up at her. The glance solidified into a full stare. Scully found herself wondering if the boy's mouth could close, or if it was permanently locked in the half-open position.

After a long pause, Scully realized that the clerk wasn't going to say "May I help you?" or "Yes?" or anything of the sort. "What's your name?" she finally asked him.

"Uh . . ." was all the clerk managed before stopping again. He gave his head a slight shake, as if to jar free the answer. Apparently it worked. "Zero," he said.

Scully nodded and smiled encouragement. "Zero, can I talk to you for a minute?"

"Sure," said Zero, smiling dimly. "What about?" Scully reached into the pocket of her jacket and pulled out her wallet.

"I'm with the FBI," she said, flashing her ID.

She watched the remaining color drain from Zero's already pallid face.

"Cool," he squeaked.

Scully put her wallet away. "Were you working here last night?"

Zero nodded. "Sure. Every night."

"Do you recognize this person?" She held up a photograph.

Zero studied the picture, wrinkling his brow. He appeared to be thinking very, very hard. "Nah," he finally answered, "never seen him."

Scully was amused by this transparent performance—but also perplexed.

"Why don't you take a closer look," she said. "He was here last night between eleven and eleven thirty . . ."

Zero slowly shook his head, as though this information meant nothing to him. As though he didn't even speak English.

Scully was getting a little annoyed now. *If someone is going to lie to me,* she thought, *it should at least be a little believable.* "He was killed in the parking lot," she continued, pointing through the front door of the arcade. The crippled car was plainly visible from where Zero stood. "That was his car. If you were here at this counter, you must have seen it happen."

"Oh," Zero said slowly. His eyes widened and his head bobbed up and down. It was a laughable parody of someone suddenly realizing the truth. *"That . . ."* he said, pointing at the car in the lot, then at the picture in Scully's hand, "was *him?*"

In the bowels of the arcade, Mulder passed row upon row of video game machines. In his suit and tie, he couldn't have been more out of place among the teenage mall rats who stood glassy-eyed in front of their machines.

Mulder passed a classic Wurlitzer jukebox fitted with compact discs. Its flashing lights and glass tubing seemed almost demure and understated in comparison to the garish games that surrounded it.

As he continued down a row of games, something on one of the screens caught his eye. He stopped in front of the Virtual Massacre II machine. The video display scrolled through the list of high scores and initials, along with the dates and times the scores had been achieved.

Mulder blinked and the scrolling list of letters and numbers suddenly disappeared, replaced by an intense scene of animated violence. A fighter's finishing move brought a shower of blood from the open mouth of his opponent. At the same time, a synthesized voice murmured, *"Come on. I know you have a quarter in your pocket . . ."*

"Last I saw, that Hammond dude fed a bunch of quarters into this one."

Mulder glanced up. The teenage attendant was leading Scully to the same machine he was staring at.

"Next thing I knew," Zero continued, "the ambulance showed up."

Scully threw Mulder a curious glance. But Mulder kept his eyes glued to the screen, waiting for the list of high scores to flash back on.

Scully turned back to Zero. "Before the ambulance showed up, did you notice anything unusual outside?"

Zero shook his head, staring blankly ahead. "It's hard to tell. I mean, the place gets pretty loud, and all. Kinda hard to hear much of anything."

Scully pressed. "Did you notice anyone else around who might have seen something?"

"I, uh . . . can't . . . I don't really remember."

Mulder let his eyes move over to the kid. He was trying too hard, Mulder thought. Whom was he protecting? And why? Mulder's eyes went back to the screen when he saw the high scores displayed there again.

"Hey! Where's the change geek?" someone deep in the arcade yelled.

" 'Scuse me," Zero said quickly, clearly relieved to have an excuse to hurry away.

"Scully, take a look at this," Mulder said, pointing to the screen.

"What?" Scully looked at the display.

"What were the names of the other victims?"

Scully opened the file and flipped to the list.

"Billy Kolbrenner . . . Ralph Sherman . . . Darin Oswald . . . Leon—"

"Darin Oswald—does he have a middle name?"

Scully checked. "Yes. Peter."

Mulder said, "Darin Peter Oswald. Let me guess—of the five victims, he was the only one who survived. Right?"

Scully checked and nodded. "Yes. How did you know?"

"Look," Mulder said, pointing to the list of high scores on the video display. The same three initials preceded every entry on the list. D.P.O. "Darin. Peter. Oswald."

Mulder touched the glass with his finger, pointing at the high scorer's initials. He traced his finger along the screen to the date, and maybe the exact time, of Jack Hammond's death.

"He was here when Hammond died."

Chapter FOUR

With a Walkman clamped on his head, Darin Peter Oswald did his work beneath the belly of a Buick. He was a fair mechanic, but then so were half the other kids in town. Maybe that was why Mr. Kiveat only paid him minimum wage.

Darin adjusted his back against the dolly he was lying on. Turning his head to reach for a wrench, he saw a sleek pair of legs enter the garage.

The corner of his mouth turned up in a grin. He'd know those legs anywhere. He had studied them more than he'd studied anything else at school.

High-heeled shoes that never seemed to pick up the dust from town strolled toward him across the stained concrete of the garage. He pushed himself out from under the Buick.

Startled, she took a step backward as Darin stood up. He quickly pulled the Walkman from his ears and adjusted his baseball cap to hide the scar.

"Hey, Mrs. Kiveat," he said, offering a gentle smile.

"Darin, you scared me," she said.

He didn't know what to say. The last thing he wanted to do was scare her.

"I'm sorry, Mrs. Kiveat," he said, looking into her eyes. They had to be the most beautiful eyes in the whole county. Heck, she had to be the most beautiful woman in the whole state. She was perfect.

He looked down at his hands. They were covered with grease. They were always covered with grease.

"Where's Frank?" she asked.

The question caught Darin a bit off guard. For some reason, he'd thought she might have come to talk to *him*. At least, that was what he had hoped.

"Frank's out on a tow," he said.

He couldn't help staring at her face. He sensed that it made her uncomfortable, but he just couldn't help himself. *A face that pretty is like a work of art,* thought Darin.

"Is there anything I can help you with?" he asked.

"No," said Mrs. Kiveat. "We were just supposed to have lunch."

Darin thought quickly. He could offer her something, couldn't he? She'd like that.

"If you're hungry," he said, "I can get you something to eat. Would you like something? I got jelly doughnuts," he said with a smile. "They're from yesterday, but they're still good. I had one."

Darin must have taken a step forward because she shook her head and stepped away.

Darin knew why.

"Uh, Mrs. Kiveat . . . ," he said, turning his gaze down to his dirty Nikes, which were painfully close to her spotless shoes. "About those things I said yesterday, I . . . uh . . ."

A tow truck turned into the garage. Frank Kiveat, his boss and her husband, drove in.

At the sight of the tow truck, Darin took two healthy steps backward.

Frank hopped out of the cab of his truck. He was tall, handsome, and friendly. *So?* thought Darin. *I can be friendly, too.*

"Sorry I'm late, hon. I had to tow that poor pizza delivery kid's car."

Darin watched closely as she gave Frank a kiss. He always watched when Mrs. Kiveat kissed her husband. Each time it seemed to Darin that the world grew just a little bit darker.

He turned away, unable to watch anymore. What made Frank so great anyway?

"Hey, Darin," Frank called out. "I just got a call on the radio. Some people are coming to see you. They say they're with the FBI."

Darin nodded solemnly and shrugged, giving nothing away.

"FBI, huh?" he said. "Maybe they need a good mechanic."

Frank chuckled slightly. Darin threw one last glance at the beautiful Mrs. Kiveat before shuffling over to the tool rack.

"So this is the dude who died, huh?"

Darin examined the photograph of Jack Hammond in better days. Yearbook photo, it looked like—perfect hair, big smile like he owned the world. Darin hated guys like that. It made him all the more glad about what he had done.

"That's pretty harsh," he said.

Although Mulder had given him the picture, Darin handed it back to Scully. Darin couldn't even keep eye contact with her, so he went back to organizing his tools.

"How did it happen?" he asked, keeping up his act as best he could.

"They say he was struck by lightning," said Mulder.

Darin couldn't help laughing at that. "Yeah, that happens," he said, popping a piece of gum into his mouth.

"Right outside the video arcade," continued

Mulder. "Not a cloud in the sky, from what we can tell."

Mulder looked at him like he could see right through him. It made Darin uncomfortable. *Must be some dumb FBI trick, or something,* he thought.

"You were there last night, weren't you?" asked Mulder.

"Oh, yeah," said Darin, figuring the fewer lies he told, the better.

"Then you must have seen something."

Darin shook his head. "Man, when I'm into my game—I'm there, you know? You could have a nucular explosion, right? I wouldn't even notice."

Darin threw a glance at Scully, who also possessed that see-through-you kind of look.

Mulder went on. "Darin, can I ask you a personal question? Do you consider yourself lucky?"

"Me?" asked Darin. "Lucky?" He suddenly figured that these FBI folks were far less intelligent than they seemed. "No, I don't think so."

"Well, I was thinking of all the people who were hit by lightning here," said Mulder. "And you're the only one who's still alive. Don't you think that's lucky?"

Darin could feel the scar on his head starting to itch just at the mention of it. That lightning had

30

burned quite a gash in him, but in the end it left him alive—very much alive.

"Yeah, well, I guess if you look at it like that, you could be right. Maybe I am lucky."

Darin was beginning to feel just a bit hot under the questioning. And that gave him an idea . . .

"Mulder," said Scully, a look of concern on her face as she came closer.

Smoke was wafting up from Mulder's jacket pocket.

Darin chewed harder on his gum to keep himself from grinning.

Mulder reached under his coat and pulled out a cellular phone that was smoking like a cigarette.

"What happened?" asked Scully.

"I don't know." Mulder gasped and dropped the hot phone. As it hit the floor, its plastic casing began to melt. Smoke poured from the device as it continued to self-destruct.

Mulder rubbed his burned hand. "It just got hot all of a sudden."

Darin glanced down at the ruined phone and shook his head. "Hmm . . . modern technology," he said. He looked up at Mulder. "I'm gonna go now. Got work to do."

The two agents looked through him again, but

with less control than they had when they'd arrived.

"Sure," said Mulder. "Thanks for your help."

"No problem," said Darin as he ambled out of the garage.

Chapter FIVE

The small bungalow Darin Oswald and his mom called home was the greatest eyesore on the block. Its paint was peeling, and it leaned to one side. Weeds had grown up around the front steps and even in the driveway. The junk that littered their yard seemed old enough to have been from another civilization.

When Darin arrived home, his mom sat hypnotized by the tube, as was her way. Roughly the same size as the couch she lay on, she stared blank-eyed at the TV. She was watching a talk-show host questioning some freak about one thing or another. As Darin peered in from the doorway behind her, the channel changed to MTV.

Darin's mom turned her head and shouted over her shoulder, "Quit foolin' with the remote!"

But even as she said it, her hand was reaching down automatically. She felt the remote wedged in between her body and the sofa and gave her son a puzzled look.

Darin was too busy guzzling down a quart of chocolate milk to notice. She kept her eyes on him as she changed the channel back to the freak show.

"Why do you watch that stuff, anyway?" asked Darin. "They're all a bunch of losers."

"At least they're on TV," she sneered. "I don't see *you* on TV."

Darin belched long and loud in response.

His mom shook her head. "Manners don't cost, Darin. They're free. What girl's ever gonna want a belching fool like you?"

"You'd be surprised," he answered.

But his mother had already turned her attention back to the tube and the parade of sideshow acts. One thing was for sure—Darin was never going to turn himself into a sideshow act. He was too smart for that. He had better plans.

Plans that included Mrs. Kiveat. She was the only person worth anything in Darin's life. She'd never dismissed him like the others. She'd never called him stupid. She'd smiled at his jokes in class. She even wrote stuff on his papers. Things to encourage him. Things to show him how much she cared about who he was, and who he could be. She made him feel like he was worth something.

Zero's trademark knock resounded on the door, pulling Darin out of his thoughts. Before Darin turned to go, he took one last look at his mom's TV.

Suddenly the screen filled with static. So much for the talk-show weirdos.

Darin stormed out of the house and across the yard. Zero struggled to keep up.

"You won't believe it, man," Zero said. "You won't *believe* who came by today."

"Let me guess," said Darin. "The FBI?"

Zero stopped in his tracks. "How did you know?"

Darin shook his head. He was constantly amazed at how dense Zero could be.

"They came to the garage," he said.

"They did? How'd they find you?"

"You tell me," Darin said between gritted teeth. "You must've said something."

Darin picked up the pace again. Zero, already out of breath, fought to keep up with him.

"No, man, I didn't say squat."

They were out in the field now. The pasture beyond Darin's home was dense and green this time of year. The land had once belonged to Darin's family—his grandfather, to be exact. But the family had lost it. Just like they lost everything else.

Darin hopped the barbed-wire fence while Zero squeezed between the wire.

"Wait up!"

Darin climbed toward the top of the hill.

"Come on, man," called Zero. "You know I wouldn't do that to you."

At the top of the hill was a little plateau where a gathering of uninterested cows slept. It still amazed Darin that cows could sleep standing up.

"I think you wanna be someplace else right now," Darin told Zero, " 'cause I'm in the mood for a little barbecue."

Zero took a deep, shuddering breath. "No, man, not the cows again."

Darin threw him a huge grin.

"Come on, don't do this. Not now," Zero begged.

Zero's reaction only made Darin laugh. Zero was so dang funny when he tried to talk Darin out of things.

Around them, they could hear the awakened cows beginning to moo, unaware of what was to come.

Darin strode away from Zero and turned his eyes to the skies—skies so clear that he could pinpoint each and every star. Suddenly the wind started blowing. Tiny clouds began to build between Darin and the moon.

The clouds began to glow bright blue as they swelled and filled with a static charge.

"Okay, I'm listening," said Darin, looking up

toward the sky. "I'm ready for you, so come on down!"

In a few moments the clouds blotted out the stars. The cows started to moo more loudly in the howling wind. Up above, thunderheads began to flash faintly.

"I'm outa here!" shouted Zero. He took off, racing from the hill, pumping his legs as fast as he could.

"Let's go, man! I'm waiting!" Darin screamed to the sky. "Let's go!"

Darin stretched his arms wide, still staring at the angry clouds.

"Come get me! I'm right here! I'm waiting!" He threw his hands high into the sky.

"Come on! Talk to me!"

The sky exploded in a barrage of lightning bolts.

All around him, the cows were fried as the lightning tore through them. *WHAM!*—a single bolt, the most powerful of all, struck Darin himself. Surging through his forehead into his transformed brain, the electricity shot down through his fingertips and out through his toes to the ground.

It burned. But at the same time, it was more wonderful than anything to feel such power.

Darin collapsed to the ground as the lightning subsided. He was exhausted by the ordeal. Yet as he lay there, he could feel the power filling him. He could feel it running through his veins, but his body was still in shock, barely able to move.

Zero came running back. He leaned over Darin and gasped, "Dude! Are you okay, man?"

Darin sat up. He could feel the electricity sparking in his earring, and in the fillings in his teeth. He could feel the charge in the air all around him. It felt like being in the center of the universe.

"I'm excellent," he said.

Chapter SIX

Sheriff Teller strode past a dead cow whose open eyes seemed to express surprise at its sudden end. He held a cellular phone up to his ear—one of the Connerville Sheriff's Department's few concessions to modernization.

Project Director Dean Greiner, his longtime friend from the Astadourian Lightning Observatory, was on the other end, giving him the rundown on the previous night's lightning storm.

"Um-hm . . . uh-huh . . . ," Teller grunted in agreement. Then he saw Scully and Mulder drive up in a dark sedan.

"Can you fax that over to my office?" he asked into the phone as he started in the direction of the agents' car. "Right away, if you can? Thanks, Dean."

Teller closed the phone and slid it into his pocket. As he swaggered over to where the two FBI agents were emerging from their car, he passed another dead cow. Flies buzzed over this one.

Teller couldn't help feeling a little embarrassed. To tell the truth, his job never got much more interesting than this. Connerville didn't have a crime rate so much as a crime trickle. The occasional drunk and disorderly, the rare vandalism call. It wasn't that Connerville citizens were so upstanding—just that there was nothing left in the town worth stealing.

Still, it was his turf, and he wasn't about to roll over without a fight.

As Scully approached across the field, she could almost smell Teller's attitude wafting toward them.

"What's happened here, Sheriff?" she asked.

Teller gestured at the animals lying on the grass. "Three dead cows." He couldn't keep his lips from curling into a smile as he asked, "How do you think they died?"

"Lightning?" Mulder asked.

Sheriff Teller nodded. "That's right. I just talked to Dean Greiner at the observatory, which is about a mile through those woods." He pointed past the agents.

Mulder turned to look and narrowed his eyes— as if trying to see it through the trees.

"Did they report lightning last night?" Scully asked.

"They can detect every lightning flash on the planet," Teller said. "Each one emits radio waves at the exact same frequency—"

"The Schuman Resonance," Mulder interjected,

swinging back around to face the sheriff. "Eight cycles per second. You can pick it up on a transistor radio."

Sheriff Teller was obviously brought up short by the interruption. He took a good, long look at Mulder.

Mulder smiled. "See that, Sheriff? I did my homework."

Sheriff Teller didn't seem impressed. "There's not much question that lightning killed these cows last night," he said. "Just like it killed Jack Hammond. And those other kids."

Mulder crouched over the dead cow at their feet. "Well, that's certainly the way it *looks*," he said.

"That's the way it *is*," Teller responded. "Let me show you something else."

Teller walked a few yards away, toward a bare patch of ground that showed through the grass of the meadow. Scully and Mulder followed. Teller kicked away some dirt from the bare patch.

"See this?" Teller gestured with his foot toward the ground. "You know what this is? Huh?" He took a deep breath, ready to explain all about the black rootlike form embedded in there.

"Looks like a fulgurite," Mulder said, stooping low to examine it.

Sheriff Teller whipped around and glared at him.

"That only happens with lightning," Mulder

went on. "When sandy soil fuses into glass from the heat of a discharge."

Sheriff Teller nodded. "How much more proof do you need? Hmmm?"

Mulder said nothing but brushed more dirt away from the fulgurite.

Teller continued, "I'd say your business here is finished." And with that he turned and headed for his car.

Scully turned to her partner. "Mulder," she began tentatively, "I have to say . . . I think he's right."

"You think we're wasting our time?" Mulder asked, working his fingers under the cold, hard substance on the ground. "That we're chasing lightning?"

"Look at the evidence. What else could it be?"

"I don't know yet." Mulder grunted as he applied pressure to the fulgurite, lifting one end of it out of the earth. With a sharp crack, a long piece of the black glass broke off in his hands. Brushing off some loose dirt, he held it out to Scully.

"But this is the first lightning strike I've ever seen that left behind a footprint."

Scully looked closer. Embedded deep in the rough, black glass, she could see unmistakable jagged tread marks.

The partial imprint of a shoe.

She rubbed her hand across it to prove it was real, not just a trick of the light. Then she turned to Mulder, but his mind was already somewhere else.

"Why don't you go to the forensics lab and get a cast of that print," he suggested as he again peered into the woods. "I'll catch up with you later."

Chapter SEVEN

"What can you tell me about lightning in Connerville?"

"Only that it strikes all the time, all year round."

Agent Mulder was met in the large atrium of the Astadourian Lightning Observatory by Dr. Dean Greiner. The building was nestled deep within a grove of tall oak trees, hidden from view. Its flat, sterile appearance was offset by a strange apparatus on the roof—something halfway between a radar antenna and a microwave transmitter. The roof was spread with a cluster of lightning rods and looked like an immense bed of nails.

Inside, an ornate atrium housed displays on the history of electricity. It was the type of gallery that schoolchildren would gawk at, but Mulder suspected no schoolchildren were invited here.

Greiner smiled through his graying beard. "The clouds are always rumbling around here," he told Mulder.

"And why is that?"

Greiner raised his eyebrows. "That's what we try to find out."

44

Mulder glanced up through the skylight. Even the pinnacle of the skylight had a lightning rod attached. Through the glass, Mulder caught sight of the bulky apparatus that adorned the roof.

"Are all those rods necessary?"

"Lightning is unpredictable," Greiner explained. "The more rods, the more likely it is to find its way to us."

Greiner began to stroll among the displays in the atrium. Mulder followed him, taking note of the variety of lightning bolts described there. A *Tesla coil* seemed to pull electricity out of the air. A *Jacob's ladder* sent a blue surge arcing up two parallel stalks. Greiner seemed proud of this place, and rightly so. Mulder wondered if he was also protective of it.

"How about that device on the roof?" Mulder asked.

Greiner hesitated for an brief instant. "Chemical storage," he finally answered. "A wet cell."

Mulder was genuinely surprised. "You mean it's a battery?"

Greiner gestured to the atrium around them. "This facility is powered by lightning, Mr. Mulder. It strikes our rods, and we harness it. Not too efficiently, of course, but we're working on that."

"And what about when the lightning doesn't strike your rods?" Mulder asked.

When he heard the question, Greiner turned slowly back to Mulder. He examined Mulder, his attitude suddenly changing.

"Despite what the townsfolk might think, we don't make the lightning. We just study it," he said coolly. "We had nothing to do with any of the tragedies that have happened in this town. The lightning was here long before we were."

Mulder backed off a bit, but the guarded look remained on Greiner's face.

"I realize that," Mulder said. "I was just wondering if you kept records of lightning victims. Not just here in Connerville, but international records as well."

Greiner shrugged and waved the question aside. "They're just numbers in our computer. I can't see what use they'd be to you."

"I'd like to see your records on people who have been struck more than once and survived," said Mulder. "To see if there's anything they might have in common."

At first Greiner seemed threatened by the request; then he broke out in laughter. Mulder couldn't tell whether he was genuinely amused or was laughing to cover his concern.

"Agent Mulder," said Greiner, "we are an understaffed, underfunded *scientific* institute. If you're looking for some sort of voodoo, you're in the wrong place."

Mulder glanced at a bronze statue of Zeus hurling a lightning bolt. Even myths sometimes had basis in fact. "I'm talking science too, Dr. Greiner. Logical explanations for things we can't understand."

Greiner offered him only a tight shrug and his empty, upturned palms. "Well, it looks like your quest has led you back to the drawing board. I'm sorry, but we don't have the answers you're looking for."

Mulder couldn't tell yet if the doctor was an enemy, but he certainly wasn't an ally.

"Thank you for your time, Dr. Greiner."

Mulder took a few steps, but before he left he turned back to Greiner.

"And by the way, this is an amazing facility you have here," Mulder said, brushing his hands across a polished brass railing. "No one would ever guess that you were 'underfunded.'"

Back in the forensics lab at the Wharton County Building, Scully waited for the fulgurite cast to dry. She checked the plaster and found it ready just as Mulder arrived. *Well,* she thought, *at least this is something real we can follow up on.* She gently pulled the casting from the fulgurite and turned it over. It revealed a perfect copy of the part of the shoe that had been captured in glass.

"Considering it's a partial imprint," she told Mulder, "there's a lot of information here."

She picked up a brush and swept away some loose crumbs of plaster and dirt.

"The tread looks like a standard military boot . . . men's . . ." She took a closer look. "Size eight and a half."

Mulder was impressed. "Eight and a half? That's pretty good, Scully."

Scully looked at her partner impishly. She knew that Mulder appreciated her, but he was so rarely impressed that for a brief moment she considered not telling him the truth. But as usual, her integrity won the day. "It says it right here on the bottom," she said, showing him where the shoe size was imprinted on the sole.

Mulder smiled. "Too bad. And I was going to tell Skinner you deserved a raise."

"Well, I have something even better," she continued. She reached for a small plastic jar. "When I was cleaning the imprint to take the mold, I found trace amounts of a thick liquid embedded in the fulgurite."

She handed the tiny jar to Mulder, and he held it up to the light.

"What is it?" he asked, looking at the green droplet.

"I'd have to conduct a chemical analysis to be sure, but it looks like antifreeze."

Mulder nodded as a few of the puzzle pieces fell into place for him. "Darin Oswald," he said.

Scully had to agree—then caught herself. "But how?"

"I don't know, Scully," Mulder responded. "But let's go see if the shoe fits."

Chapter EIGHT

A single traffic light hung on a wire above the intersection of County Road A-7 and Connerville Pass. It used to be a four-way stop, which should have been good enough for a crossroads out in the middle of nowhere. But over the years, too many people had died thinking a stop sign was just an option. So the county had seen fit to put in the traffic light.

The funny thing was, it didn't make much of a difference. And in fact, the accidents had increased over the past couple of months.

On this particularly dreary day, two cars were speeding down the roads. The brown Chrysler had the green light. It didn't even slow down as it headed toward the intersection. As for the blue Impala, it had been decelerating—but the driver punched the accelerator when the light turned green. Although the drivers couldn't see it, the light had just gone green in all four directions.

They both barreled through the intersection. The silence of the quiet crossroads was violated by the sudden screech of tires. The two cars spun out of control, trying to avoid a lethal collision.

Fate took a hand in this one, and the two cars missed each other by a fraction of an inch.

"What's your problem? Are you crazy!"

"You think you own the whole road?"

The two drivers screamed at each other. Then they sped off even more furiously than they had entered the intersection.

Darin Oswald chuckled to himself. From where he sat, on the edge of an abandoned billboard, it was like being in the grandstand at the demolition derby. But this little game of Red Light–Green Light was a lot more fun than that. You never knew how people were going to react. And since Darin knew most of the people who came through the intersection, it gave him a special thrill each time he played.

Darin wasn't mean to everyone—just the people who deserved it. Like all those classmates who had treated him like pond scum. And all the shopkeepers who eyed him suspiciously whenever he walked into their stores. And all the townsfolk who'd smile at his face and call him names behind his back. Everyone did—he knew it. As far as Darin was concerned, every last one of them deserved whatever bad luck came their way. He felt no more remorse for the pizza guy he'd fried than he would for a moth that sizzled on a bug zapper.

Soon after the two cars had sped off, Darin looked down to see Zero lumbering up the rusty ladder that led to the abandoned billboard where he sat. The wooden planks of the ledge could barely hold their combined weight, but it was a good place to be. Darin had always found a sense of peace here and often came. His newfound talent had made the place even more inviting.

When he looked up, two more cars were headed toward destiny. New ones, with antilock brake systems, no doubt. *We'll just see if those fancy new brake systems really work,* Darin thought as Zero sat down beside him.

"Dude, what's happening?" said Zero. It was more his standard greeting than an actual question.

"I dunno," mumbled Darin. "Nothin'."

Darin sent out a little mind-pulse, and in the intersection, the traffic light did its Red Light–Green Light thing. A Jeep Cherokee almost broadsided a minivan. Both cars slid to a stop, honking their horns. Close, but no cigar. Darin guessed those antilock brakes must be worth something.

"I'm thinking we should go somewhere," said Zero. "Get out of this hole. Maybe check out Las Vegas." He grinned. "You could do some serious damage someplace like that."

Darin shook his head. "I'm not going to Las

Vegas. I'm not going anywhere . . . not without Mrs. Kiveat. Not without Sharon."

Just saying her name made him feel good inside, as if being able to say her first name out loud made him that much closer to her.

Zero, on the other hand, just rolled his eyes.

"What makes you think she'd go anywhere with you? She failed you, remember?" Zero reminded him. "She thinks you're a retard."

This was something Darin had thought about a lot. He had decided that just because he couldn't pass her English class didn't mean he was unworthy of her love. In the grand scheme of things, what did his book smarts matter when he had this incredible power?

"Forget school, man," Darin told Zero. "I'm talking about proving my love."

"And how are you gonna do that?"

Darin looked out over the intersection, no longer seeing the cars or the traffic light. "By letting her know how I feel. By telling her how all I ever think about is her."

In a way, Darin was glad Zero had asked. Talking about it made his determination even stronger.

"Excuse me, Romeo," Zero scoffed. "There's another slight problem. She's married to your boss."

Darin pulled his knees to his chest and crossed his arms around them. "Not a problem."

"How is that not a problem?"

"I can take care of him," Darin said with a shrug. "Maybe I can fry him."

The thought didn't seem to sit well with Zero. "Dude, he's your boss."

"Not if he's dead, he won't be." Somehow he didn't feel bad about thinking such unpleasant thoughts. Not bad at all. In fact, he wanted to giggle.

"Are you nuts?" Zero asked. "With the FBI hanging around? Just forget it, okay?" His voice was becoming serious. "You can't compete with Frank. He's good-looking, he owns his own shop, plus he *fixes* things"—Zero threw a glance at the crossroads—"instead of just busting stuff up. You think she's gonna give up a guy like him?"

Darin didn't like the direction this conversation was taking. Even more irritating was the fact that some of what Zero said made sense.

"A woman like that wants someone special," Zero persisted.

Darin couldn't look at him. "I am special."

Zero just looked away. "Yeah, right."

Off in the distance, a stake-bed truck came over the hill. On Connerville Pass, a white Ford sped toward the crossroads.

"Well," said Darin, "I'm gonna show Mrs. Kiveat just how special I am."

Zero took a good, long look at him. "How do you expect to do that?" Zero's voice seemed kind of shaky.

Darin smiled. "I got more ways than you can imagine." He turned to look at the approaching cars. Suddenly the demolition derby game took on a new importance. It didn't have to be just a game. It could be part of a plan. A brilliant, terrible, and wonderful plan. His grin broadened as he thought about it. It was the type of plan that would have gotten him an A+ in some class somewhere.

And the best part was that Sharon Kiveat would soon know just how special he could be.

Down below, the two cars closed in. Darin pushed his mind toward the traffic light, feeling his odd electrical aura tingle like a static charge. He switched the signal from red to green in both directions.

He counted down. "Five . . . four . . . three . . . two . . . one . . ."

WHAM!

The truck broadsided the Ford, crushing its passenger side and sending it spinning off the road into a ditch. The truck spun out of control, dumping its cargo of cabbages. Cabbage heads shattered on the ground and flew in all directions as the truck bounced off the road. It finally crashed into a telephone pole, where it stopped dead.

Darin laughed. "Whoa . . . that was a good one," he said, getting up. "That was a *really* good one."

Zero grinned too but didn't seem all that pleased.

Darin rapped him on the arm. "What's the matter with you, man?" But Zero didn't answer.

"Come on," Darin said. "Let's go down and check it out."

Chapter NINE

Scully and Mulder's shiny rented car was totally out of place on the crabgrass lawn of the Oswald home.

Inside, Darin's mother was showing the two agents around. At the end of the hall, she swung open a creaky door, into the stale air of her son's room.

"Darin ain't worth much, I'm the first one to say it . . . but he wouldn't hurt a soul," she told them. "What kind of trouble is he in, anyway?"

Scully and Mulder looked at one another. Better not to discuss it just yet.

"Can we have a few minutes, Mrs. Oswald?" Mulder asked gently.

The woman stepped back and let them enter. Mulder closed the door behind them.

The room was worse than the rest of the house. Even the daylight seemed cold as it filtered through the mildewed drapes. The bed was unmade. The floor was an obstacle course of car parts and dirty laundry. The ceiling featured a huge Nightwalkers poster, and the walls held a tattered collage of

Darin Oswald's solitary life. Even Darin's fish tank was a testament to despair. Scully and Mulder could see no fish in its murky depths.

Mulder examined the pictures on the wall. Most of them were cut from magazines—places Darin would never go and famous people he would never meet. A black-and-white photo, out of place among the color glossies, caught Mulder's eye. The woman pictured was as pretty as any of the models on the wall, but her smile seemed far more real.

Scully's trained eye scoured the boy's closet until she came up with a worn sneaker.

"Mulder, we've got a size match," she said.

"Eight and a half?"

She nodded. "But it doesn't prove he killed Jack Hammond."

Scully smirked as she noticed Mulder looking at the beautiful models tacked on Darin's wall. "Find anything you like?" she asked.

"I don't know," he said. "Scully, what's wrong with this picture?"

Scully reached up and pulled down the small black-and-white photo.

"Who is she?" Scully asked.

"I don't know, but it looks like some kind of year-book photo."

Scully immediately returned to the closet and

produced a yearbook she had noticed while looking for the shoe. It wasn't hard to find the page the picture was cut from. There was a name beneath the hole where the picture should have been.

"Sharon Kiveat," she said out loud.

Kiveat. The name was far too familiar.

Frank Kiveat was sipping coffee in his tow truck when the call came in. He slipped his truck into gear, stepped on the gas, and hung a left on Connerville Pass heading toward the county road.

He'd lost count of how many times he'd been down there lately, picking up the pieces after a bad accident. The last time out, he'd thought someone ought to check the conditions at the intersection, see what the problem was. He had even thought about sending a letter to the County Planning Commission.

But he wasn't thinking about any of that today. Instead he was thinking about the boy. Darin Oswald. At lunch yesterday, his wife had been nervous, jumpy. When he'd asked her why, she'd mentioned Darin's name, then changed the subject.

Frank had hired Darin at his wife's urging, months ago. Since then, he'd taken a shine to the kid. Something about Darin's awkwardness, and his hopeless lack of social skills, had brought out a fatherly protectiveness in Frank that he hadn't known he had.

But if Darin was making his wife feel uncomfortable, then that was that. The kid would have to go. Since this was Darin's day off, it gave Frank an extra day to come up with an excuse to give him. "Business is slow" wouldn't cut it, because it wasn't. He'd have to come up with something more convincing.

Frank arrived at the site of the accident shortly after the ambulances. He scanned the scene as he rolled to a stop: A late-model Ford in an open trench. An old farm truck, wrapped around a telephone pole, blocking eastbound traffic. Even out here in the middle of nowhere, a crowd had gathered to watch the action.

Frank set the parking brake and got out of his truck. He approached a deputy who was waving cars, a few at a time, through the intersection.

"What happened?" Frank asked him.

"Some kid got centerpunched," the deputy answered, looking over at Frank before returning his full attention to the job at hand. "Just got his license, too. He's pretty bad off."

"Poor kid," Frank said. It kind of put things in perspective, he thought. Maybe he'd hold off on firing Darin, at least until he'd had a chance to talk

the whole thing over with Sharon. Maybe he'd mis-
understood her. Maybe they could clear the whole
thing up if they could just—

His thoughts were shattered by a searing pain
shooting through his chest. He grimaced as he drew
in a sharp breath, then let it out slowly.

What on earth was that? he wondered, taking
another, slower breath. He realized his left shoulder
had gone numb. *Is it heartburn?* Sharon had been
asking him to lay off the greasy foods—maybe he
should start listening.

"You guys ready for me to clear the road?" he
asked the deputy in a strained voice.

"I'm just directing traffic." The deputy didn't
take his eyes off the cars rolling by. "You'd better
check with the sheriff." He gestured back toward
the farm truck, where Sheriff Teller was busy taking a statement.

Frank said nothing. The pain hadn't subsided. If
anything, it was getting worse. He rubbed his chest
harder, his breath coming in shorter bursts.

"Hey, pal," the deputy said, concerned, "are you
okay? You don't look so good."

Frank was about to admit that he didn't feel so
good, either, when a familiar face at the edge of the
crowd caught his eye.

Darin Oswald.

That's strange, Frank thought, making eye contact with him. *What's he doing here—*

Suddenly Frank felt Darin reach deep into his chest and turn up the heat from a slow burn to an inferno.

Only how could that be? Darin was twenty yards away!

Still, Frank knew, as surely as if the boy had been standing directly next to him, that Darin was killing him.

He turned to the deputy and opened his mouth to speak. All he could manage was a cry of agony as another bolt of pain hit him. The deputy caught Frank as he doubled over, his mind edging away from consciousness as he slid to the highway.

Darin watched from the sidelines along with the other spectators as the drama continued to unfold.

"Darin, what's happening?" asked Zero. But Darin just ignored him.

Frank Kiveat's heart was quivering uselessly in his chest. As he lay there on the glass-covered asphalt, the deputy called to the paramedics standing by. When they saw Frank on the ground, they came running.

Darin grinned. *Ain't nothing they can do,* he thought. *Just make fools of themselves.*

"What happened?" shouted one of the paramedics.

The deputy stood up and backed away. "He just collapsed."

Darin stepped over to the side to get a better view. The paramedic put his hand around Frank's throat, checking his pulse.

Zero just stared at the fallen Kiveat, and then at Darin, back and forth, back and forth, as if he were watching a tennis match.

"No pulse!" shouted the paramedic. "Get the kit!"

As the second paramedic ran off toward the ambulance, Darin took a deep breath and strode forward. Zero grabbed his arm.

"Hey, man, what are you doing? Let's get out of here!"

Zero was in a cold sweat. Darin just shook him off and headed out into the intersection.

By now the paramedic had ripped open Frank's shirt and put a stethoscope to his chest. The look on his face said everything. Frank was in a bad, bad way.

Darin continued to drift unnoticed around the crash site, getting closer to his dying boss. He watched as the second paramedic came flying back with the cardiac kit. By now the first guy was doing that CPR thing—external compressions—to Frank's muscular chest. But it did no good.

Working quickly, they wired electrodes onto Frank's torso. Darin could hear the single monotonous tone and see the green flatline of Frank's heart on the monitor.

"Come on!" said the paramedic, pumping on Frank's chest. "The defibrillator! Now!"

The second paramedic pulled two electronic paddles from the machine. Just like the ones Darin always saw on those hospital shows.

The paramedic put the paddles on Frank's chest. "Give me three hundred joules," he said.

"It's already charged," said the other.

"No, it's not."

They both looked at the device, which seemed about as stone dead as the man on the ground.

For Darin, draining that thing's battery had been easier than changing the traffic lights.

"Something's not working here. Go get the backup!" One paramedic raced back to the ambulance while the other tried desperately to get the kit working. He was too busy to notice as Darin came up to Frank Kiveat.

Frank's eyes fluttered. Darin didn't know if he could see him or hear him, but that didn't matter.

"Don't worry, Mr. Kiveat," Darin said calmly. "I've seen how they do it on TV."

Darin took his oil-browned fingers and spread them wide, laying them across Frank's chest. *The power of life and death is an intense thing,* Darin thought. *How cool to control it.*

He started the sparks in his mind. He could feel them building as they spun through his brain, picking up force like a wave rushing toward shore. And then he let it loose, down through his neck and shoulders. Racing through his arms and exploding from the tips of his fingers.

KER-CHUNK!

Frank's chest heaved with the electrical charge. His back arched and he rose nearly a foot into the air before coming back down to the ground. The second paramedic had arrived with the backup kit. But they wouldn't be needing that now.

Frank's heartbeat pinged loud and clear on the monitor. The flatline had changed to a regular series of blips—the kind that meant the patient was alive and well.

The paramedics just stared at Frank in disbelief. "We got a rhythm—but how?"

Only then did they notice Darin, and Darin couldn't hold back his smile. It beamed with its own special electricity.

"Rescue 911," he said.

He was a hero now. The kind of hero everyone loved.

The kind of hero Mrs. Kiveat would be awfully, awfully proud of.

Chapter TEN

Mulder stood at the nurses' station at the ICU of Connerville Community Hospital. He wanted to get in to talk to Frank Kiveat, but he was rapidly losing hope that he'd get the okay from Kiveat's doctors.

But Mulder wasn't letting the time slip away unused. He was leafing through Darin Oswald's medical file, checking out the records from the night he'd been struck by lighting.

According to his chart, Darin had been admitted to the ER five months earlier in cardiac arrest with third-degree burns on his head, neck, and back. The hospital had discovered, after he'd been there a few days, that Darin had a preexisting condition. Acute hypokalemia, it was called.

An idea began to form in Mulder's mind. He wasn't sure it made sense—and yet, somehow, it was the only thing that *did* make sense. He'd run it by Scully as soon as she came back from talking to the paramedics who had brought Kiveat in.

Mulder heard a soft, wet splash and looked up from Oswald's medical report.

Sharon Kiveat stood across the hallway at the

water cooler, staring down at the paper cup she had just dropped. A small puddle of water spread on the floor.

"Here," Mulder said before she could bend down, "let me give you a hand."

He retrieved the cup from the floor and dropped it in a nearby wastebasket. He pulled a fresh cup from the cooler, filled it. and gave it to her.

"Thank you," she said.

Mulder took a moment to remind himself that she wasn't just a piece in a puzzle, or simply a link to Frank Kiveat. She was a scared and tired woman.

"Mrs. Kiveat . . . I'm sorry about your husband."

"Thank you," she said again, looking at him more closely. Mulder could tell she was trying to figure out who he was. A friend? An acquaintance? How did he know her name?

"My name is Fox Mulder," he said. "I'm with the FBI."

She nodded in recognition. "You came to my husband's garage yesterday."

Mulder nodded too. "I know this is a hard time for you, but I'd like to ask you a few questions."

She shook her head and attempted an apologetic smile. "I'm sorry, I can't right now."

"I'd like to ask you about Darin Oswald."

Instantly her face changed. *She knows something,* Mulder thought.

"He was at the scene of the accident, wasn't he?" he asked.

The woman's eyes flashed. Mulder recognized that look. He had seen the same expression in the eyes of cornered animals. *She knows it was Oswald!* Mulder thought suddenly. *But how?*

"Please," Mrs. Kiveat finally said, "I need to see my husband." She moved past him, closing the door behind her as she entered her husband's room.

Mulder could see her through the glass window of the ICU cubicle. She took a seat in a chair next to her husband's bed. Frank Kiveat was unconscious and hooked up to a dozen machines and monitors.

At that moment, Mulder became aware of someone behind him. He spun instinctively, but it was only Scully.

"I just talked to the paramedics," she reported. "They were pretty rattled."

"Why?"

"Take a look at this." She unfolded a long, narrow strip of paper and handed it to him. "It's Frank Kiveat's electrocardiogram."

Mulder looked at the piece of paper. A long, straight line, then a sudden spike, followed by the familiar, repeating squiggle of a normal heartbeat.

"See this spike?" said Scully, pointing. "That indicates that some kind of electrical intervention started his heart."

"So?"

"According to the paramedics, the defibrillator wasn't charged. The paddles were dead."

"Then how do they explain this?" Mulder asked, fluttering the electrocardiogram.

"They can't explain it. All they saw was Darin Oswald touching Kiveat's chest."

Mulder stared at his partner. *There it is,* he thought.

"There's something I want you to take a look at," he said, striding back to the nurses' station. He picked up Darin Oswald's medical file and handed it to her. "I was going over Oswald's chart . . ."

Scully flipped open the folder and ran a finger down the handwritten comments. She nodded as she read, then stopped at one line. "This is odd. His blood tests showed acute hypokalemia."

Mulder smiled. She had noticed it, too.

"Electrolyte imbalance, right?" he asked.

"Essentially, yes."

"And don't electrolytes generate the electrical impulses in our bodies?"

"Sure, every time our heart beats, or a neuron

fires . . ." Scully trailed off and looked at him. "Why? What are you thinking?"

"Okay. It's a leap, Scully . . . but what if Oswald's electrolyte imbalance is enabling him to generate electricity at abnormally high levels?"

"How high?"

Mulder waved the electrocardiogram in his hand. "This high." He paused. "Higher."

Scully shook her head. "Mulder, the human body doesn't work like that."

Mulder took a step and ran his hand through his hair. *There's another piece,* he thought, *a piece missing. A piece of . . .*

"The fulgurite," he said, and turned back to Scully. "What if Oswald's body is more conductive than normal? That heel print we found in the fulgurite. If it was Oswald, then that means he conducted millions of volts into the ground and just walked away. But what if some of that power stayed in him—stored in his body like a battery?"

"What are you saying? That he's some kind of lighting rod?"

"No." Mulder considered his words carefully. "I'm saying that he *is* lightning. And we've got to stop him before he strikes again."

Chapter ELEVEN

Five months of living like this, knowing he had the ultimate power wired into his body.

He'd thought he was going to die when the lightning hit him. It was a freak storm, the kind no one saw coming. Least of all him.

It had been just a few months after graduation. He was crossing the fields, going back home from the video arcade one night, when the sky suddenly turned black. The winds blew fiercely and the rain blasted from the heavens, hitting him at a strange angle.

He could see the lightning playing high above, and he turned his eyes on the observatory on the top of the hill. Things got struck by lightning in Connerville all the time. But those were lightning rods up at that institute place, weren't they? They were supposed to attract the lightning away from people.

He raced across the open fields, drenched to the bone. He could see his house in the distance. He pumped his legs full speed, but the thick, wet grass sloshed beneath his heavy boots, making it hard to run.

And then—*BAM!*—the lightning came down on him, like a fist from the sky. His body exploded with such intense pain he wanted to scream, but his muscles had knotted and locked from the force of the bolt. It surged through his skull, setting his hair on fire. Then it surged out through his feet into the ground.

When he came to, it was a week later. He was all bandaged and achy in a hospital bed.

No one was with him.

Eventually his mother showed up. She cried and yelled at him for being so stupid as to run through a field in the middle of a thunderstorm.

No one else came by, not even Zero. Zero had a problem with hospitals.

But the day before he checked out, Mrs. Kiveat showed up. She brought a tin of cookies and told him that Frank needed some help down at the garage and offered him the job. That was when he vowed that someday he'd make her the happiest woman alive. He'd do whatever it took to make her happy. Whatever was necessary.

A couple of days after that, he picked up a dead flashlight. It came back to life, glowing so brightly that the bulb blew up. The batteries started oozing acid in his hands. He showed Zero how he could put a lightbulb in his mouth and it would come on. At first it just seemed funny.

But it wasn't funny anymore.

On the same afternoon that he nearly killed, then saved, Frank Kiveat, Darin Oswald climbed out of his bedroom window to evade the FBI at his door.

He felt the electricity raging inside him as he took off across the field—the same field where the bolt had first struck him. The same field where it had struck him many times since—although it hurt only the first time.

But the FBI people saw him and followed.

"Darin!" he heard the one named Mulder say. "Darin, wait!"

Mulder was hurrying after him. Darin wanted to run away, but he knew that running would do no good. He should have thought this through better. He should have waited for the FBI to leave before he stopped and then jump-started Frank Kiveat's heart. He should have done it someplace different from the accident site. It would have been less suspicious. And he should never ever have let Zero in on a single bit of it.

Zero was supposed to be his friend, but lately he was turning into a millstone around his neck.

Mulder and Scully caught up to him in the field, and Mulder grabbed his arm. Darin pulled away. He gritted his teeth, his eyes bulging in anger.

"Don't touch me, man!" he screamed. He wanted to blast them both right there, make them just go away for good and leave him alone.

But he knew he couldn't do that. It would just mean that more FBI people would show up in town. Like ants around a picnic. And they'd never leave him alone.

Mulder backed off. "Okay, all right."

"Don't ever touch me."

"We just want to talk to you, Darin," said Scully, trying to calm him down. "That's all."

"I didn't do anything," Darin said. But he knew he didn't sound too convincing.

Scully stepped forward slowly. "No one's saying you did. We just thought you might be able to answer a few questions for us. If you can, fine. If not . . ."

Darin took a deep breath. He forced down the charge that was begging to escape. He forced it deep inside, until it was little more than a smoldering fire.

"Okay," he said. "So what do you want to talk about?"

Scully sat in the interrogation room of the

county jail, watching Darin Oswald rub his eyes. He was tired, and it was such an innocent gesture that he suddenly looked much younger—almost fragile. Could his small body really harbor such destructive power, as Mulder believed? Did *she* really believe it?

Then Darin looked at her, his eyes cold, calculating. And she knew he could.

"How many times do I have to say it?" Darin asked. "I don't know how those people died."

"Why did you run when you saw us?" Scully asked.

Darin slammed his hands on the table. "I was taking a walk. That's not against the law, is it?"

"Do you usually leave through your window?"

Darin's eyes flashed dangerously. "You guys should be giving me a medal. I saved my boss's life."

Scully shook her head. This was hopeless. They'd gone over it a dozen times, and Darin Oswald wasn't changing his story. With no hard evidence, they wouldn't be able to hold him much longer.

"We're not so sure you did," she said, disappointed. She pushed back from the table and stood up.

Darin leaned back in his chair. "Why not?" he demanded as she walked to the door. "Who told you that? Who you been talking to? Did Zero tell you that?"

The deputy outside opened the door. Scully took one last look at Darin. His hands rested lightly on the edge of the table, and his small body was hunched over in his chair. He looked helpless. Until he turned around to face her. His eyes were alive, nearly painful in their intensity. They were almost . . . electric.

Scully left the room.

"What did he say?" Mulder asked as he greeted her in the hallway.

"Not much . . . except that he's a hero."

Mulder snorted. "How did he say he revived Kiveat?"

"CPR." Scully smiled wryly as she recalled Oswald's answer. "He claims he paid attention in health class."

Mulder shook his head. "I've been thinking about it, Scully. I don't think Oswald just revived Frank Kiveat. I think he set the whole thing up."

"What do you mean? You think he also caused the heart attack?"

Mulder nodded.

"Why would he do that?" Scully asked.

"I don't know," Mulder admitted, then added, "but I think I know someone who does."

Chapter TWELVE

Mulder pulled the car to a stop in front of an attractive two-story house in one of the few nice neighborhoods of Connerville.

"This is it?" Mulder asked his partner.

Scully checked the address she had jotted down and nodded.

On the way over, Mulder had told Scully about his short conversation with Sharon Kiveat.

A moment after they rang the bell, Sharon Kiveat opened the door. If she had come home from the hospital to rest, it hadn't helped. She looked, if anything, more exhausted than before.

She took one look at the two agents and her face froze.

"Mrs. Kiveat—" Mulder began, but the woman cut him off.

"I'm sorry. I can't do this now. I'm just leaving for the hospital." It looked to Scully as if Mrs. Kiveat was about to break into tears.

"Darin Oswald is in custody, Mrs. Kiveat," Mulder said to her. "We picked him up this afternoon."

The woman just looked at them.

"But we can't press criminal charges," Scully added, "without your help."

Scully studied the woman's face. Mulder was right—Sharon Kiveat did know something about Oswald. Scully could also see that, in spite of her fear, she wanted to tell someone.

"May we come in?" Scully asked gently.

Mrs. Kiveat hesitated for a moment, then opened the door wider to let them in.

As the two agents entered the Kiveats' living room, Scully noted the tasteful furniture—white upholstery and carpets, accented by plants in antique pots. Sharon Kiveat's delicate hand was evident everywhere in the room, along with something else: a comforting warmth. Scully knew, instinctively, that the two people who lived in this house were very happy.

But not right now. Not tonight.

"I teach remedial reading at the high school," Mrs. Kiveat said as they sat down. "Darin was my student."

"How would you describe your relationship with him?" Scully asked.

"Well, I'm not blind. I knew he had a crush on me," Mrs. Kiveat said. "But I . . . I felt sorry for him."

She shrugged and looked a little embarrassed, as though she had violated some unwritten law against caring. "I just thought he'd had more than his share of bad luck."

"So you got him the job at your husband's garage?"

Mrs. Kiveat nodded. "Then, a few months ago . . . I started getting these phone calls. Someone would call and then hang up."

"What made you think it was Darin?" Scully asked.

Mrs. Kiveat frowned, making a visible effort to put the feeling into words. "The way he looked at me in the garage . . . the phone calls made me feel the same way." She looked at Scully, then Mulder. "And I just knew."

Scully believed her, but belief wasn't enough. So far, Mrs. Kiveat hadn't given them anything they could hand a judge.

"When did you first suspect that Darin was involved with more than just prank calls?" asked Mulder.

Mrs. Kiveat looked directly at Mulder. "He told me."

Scully leaned forward. "He actually confessed to killing those people?"

VOLTAGE

"No," she said slowly. "But he told me he had powers. Dangerous powers."

Scully nodded, encouraging her to go on. They were so close now.

"When did he say this?" asked Mulder.

"Just a few days ago. After that boy was killed."

"Jack Hammond?" Scully asked.

Mrs. Kiveat nodded and looked down. "I didn't believe him. I thought he was just mouthing off, trying to impress me in some sick way. But after what happened today . . ." She raised her eyes to meet Scully's. "I knew it was true. Everything he said—he could do."

"Have you told anyone else this?" Mulder asked.

Mrs. Kiveat smiled, a small, sad smile, and shook her head. "Who would have believed me?"

Mulder nodded sympathetically.

"And I was afraid," Mrs. Kiveat continued. "I was afraid of what he would do to me . . . and . . . and what he would do to my husband."

She raised a hand to her mouth.

Scully moved closer and put a comforting hand on her shoulder. "Well, you don't have to be afraid anymore. You and your husband are safe . . . as long as we can count on your testimony."

The tears flowed from Sharon Kiveat's eyes. She

nodded, accepting the warmth of Scully's hand and the promise of her words.

On their way back to the county jail, Mulder and Scully discussed the best strategy for placing a live wire like Darin Peter Oswald under arrest.

"I don't know how fast he is with this thing," Mulder cautioned, adding with a grin, "he might be as quick as greased—"

"Don't say it," Scully said, the corners of her mouth turning upward in spite of herself. But she checked her gun anyway. It was loaded and ready.

They arrived at the jail a few minutes later, ready for anything.

Except what they found.

As they walked through the door of the interrogation room, they saw a deputy at the table, flipping through a magazine. Except for him, the room was empty.

"Where's Oswald?" Mulder asked.

"Did you transfer him to a cell?" Scully asked.

"I sent him home." The voice came from behind them, and the two agents turned to see Sheriff Teller.

"You *released* him?" Mulder asked in disbelief.

"After I read your report," the sheriff shot back, waving the file in his hand.

Mulder glanced at Scully. "I'm going to call Sharon Kiveat," he said, pushing past the sheriff.

Scully followed the sheriff into the hall as he opened the file and began reading aloud. " 'Homicide by emission of direct electric current'?" He scowled up at Scully. "You don't honestly believe this?"

Scully crossed her arms and narrowed her eyes at the big man. "I believe that Darin Oswald was involved—*in some way*—in the deaths of those four people . . . and I believe it was irresponsible of you to let him go."

The sheriff shook his head, chuckling in that folksy way of his. "Now let me get this straight. You're telling me that kid's throwing lightning bolts."

Scully took the plunge. "In effect. Yes."

The sheriff dropped the folksy act. He slapped the file shut and sputtered, " 'In effect'? There's no possible basis for that claim. Of all the wild speculation—"

"You said yourself, Sheriff," Scully said, "even scientists can't explain how lightning works."

The sheriff opened his mouth, but no sound came out, so he closed it again.

Mulder came running back down the hall. "Sharon Kiveat's not home," he called, out of breath.

"She must be on her way to the hospital," Scully answered. The two agents raced back down the hall, leaving the sheriff alone to consider what he'd unleashed.

Chapter THIRTEEN

For once in his life, Bart "Zero" Liquori was happy to be working. Night shifts at the arcade kept his mind happily away from thoughts of Darin Oswald and the dangerous games he'd been playing lately.

Not that Bart didn't like a little twisted stuff himself now and again, but what Darin was up to was miles beyond twisted. It was evil. And Zero just did not want to think about it.

A guy and his girlfriend exhausted their quarters at the air hockey game and left at ten minutes to twelve. Zero sat alone, reading a comic book. At midnight he went to the main breaker and shut down the power. The arcade fell into dark silence.

Well, not quite silence. On the other side of the arcade, a single screen switched on. A familiar theme played from the machine. Zero cautiously crept forward to see the Virtual Massacre II game. Superimposed over its animated fighters were the top twenty scores. D.P.O. D.P.O. D.P.O.

"Dude?" Zero waited for a response but got none. "Darin, I know it's you. I mean, it's gotta be you."

Still no answer.

Then the jukebox came on full blast. The Nightwalkers.

The whole scene was sickeningly familiar to Zero. He laughed nervously.

"Come on, dude, what's the deal?" Zero made his way to the door, trying to hold down his panic. The air around him felt thick and heavy. It smelled ionized. Like the air after a lightning storm.

With each step he took, Zero felt his legs grow weaker, but he knew it was only his own terror. He felt like he was trying to swim away from a shark that he knew was somewhere beneath him, but he couldn't see.

He pushed at the front door, but it didn't give. He'd already locked it. He pulled the keys out of his pocket, desperately trying in the dim light to find the right one and insert it into the lock. But his hands were shaking so badly he couldn't do it.

"What are you doing?" he cried. "I said I didn't tell them!"

Only the blasting music answered him.

Finally he got the key into the lock, opened the door, and barreled out into the windy night. But even out in the parking lot, the music blared, as if the trees themselves had turned into speakers, pulsating heavy metal.

The wind whipped around him, but still there was no sign of Darin. "I didn't say nothing! I swear!" screamed Zero, bursting into tears like a little kid. "Why are you doing this, man? We're buddies."

Zero finally got his answer. Louder than the music and brighter than the sun, a bolt of power struck him in the back. It tore through his heart and out of his chest into the ground.

Quarters flew from his pockets as he fell. But he never heard them, because he was dead before he hit the asphalt.

Standing on the roof of the arcade, Darin Oswald gazed down at the twisted figure of his friend lying in the parking lot.

He tried to dig down deep inside himself and find the slightest hint of remorse for what he had just done to his best and only friend. But he felt nothing. It was as if the electricity had burned the conscience right out of him. There was no turning back now. No stopping what he had started. He would see this through to its brutal end.

As long as Mrs. Kiveat was with him, it would all have been worth it.

Everything would be okay.

Darin turned off the music that was blaring in the jukebox and in the wind around him.

Over his head, a storm built to the north, preparing to bear down on the town.

Darin didn't notice. He had other things on his mind. He climbed down from the roof to collect Zero's body.

Chapter FOURTEEN

All the way to the hospital, Scully wished that Mulder, who was already driving as fast as he could, would drive even faster.

They had given Sharon Kiveat their word that she and her husband would be safe. Scully wasn't about to let Darin Oswald, or Sheriff Teller, make her into a liar.

When Mulder pulled up in front of the hospital, Scully was out of the car before it had rolled to a stop.

Inside, Scully pounded the button for the elevator. She was about to take the stairs when Mulder and the elevator arrived simultaneously.

When they got to the fifth floor, she blew through the elevator doors as soon as they were open.

Mulder flashed his ID at the startled ICU nurse as Scully kept moving to the end of the hall. "Call Security," Mulder commanded. "Have them deny entry to the hospital to anyone except emergency personnel."

He caught up to Scully at the door of Kiveat's

room. Through the window, they could see Sharon Kiveat. She was unharmed and looking as relaxed as possible under the circumstances, sitting by the still figure of her husband.

Scully let out a small sigh of relief and opened the door to the room.

"Sharon," she said softly.

Sharon looked up, alarmed. "What is it?" She stood up and walked toward the door.

"We need you to come with us right away," Scully answered.

"Why? What's wrong?"

Mulder answered. "Darin Oswald. He was released from custody."

"But how?" Sharon took an involuntary step backward, looking from one agent to the other. "You said we didn't have to worry, that we were safe."

"I know," Scully said. "We don't have much time. Come with us, and we'll explain—"

But Sharon shook her head. "The doctor said my husband can't be moved. I'm not leaving him."

Mulder stepped forward and spoke intently. "I'll stay with him. You go with Agent Scully."

"No," Sharon Kiveat said firmly.

"Sharon, please,"

The lights went off. After what was probably half

a second but seemed much longer, the emergency power kicked in, bathing the hospital in dim light.

Mulder looked around and drew his gun. "He's here," he said softly.

The three of them heard a soft *ping* from far down the hall. Scully craned her neck around Mulder, searching for the source of the sound. The brightest light in the corridor came from the row of lights over the elevator door.

The elevator was coming up.

Mulder and Scully ran toward the elevator. *Ping*. It was on the fourth floor now—just beneath them. They stopped at the elevator, assumed firing stance, and cocked their weapons, aiming at the black crack between the two elevator doors.

Ping.

The elevator doors started to open. Scully tensed her finger on the trigger, staring down the gunsight. There was someone inside the elevator. He was lying in a crumpled heap on the floor.

Scully and Mulder lowered their guns. Scully realized who it was. The kid from the video arcade. Zero.

She moved into the elevator and knelt by the body, feeling for a pulse on his neck. Why . . .

Suddenly Darin's final remark in the interrogation room came back to her, but it was too late for her to do anything about it.

"He's dead," she told Mulder.

Mulder reached into the elevator and pulled out the Stop switch to hold the car on that floor.

The nurse on duty stepped up behind him. "Oh, Lord," she said, seeing the body.

Mulder turned to her. "What are the other entry points to this floor?"

The nurse pointed to the far end of the hall, also shrouded in darkness. "Just the stairway," she said, still trying to pull herself together.

Mulder turned to Scully. "Stay with the Kiveats," he said, already moving toward the stairs.

"But Mulder—" she began.

"I'm going after Oswald." Then he was gone.

Mulder pushed through the door to the stairwell and paused to let his eyes adjust to the light. Backup lights were on in here too, but these were bloodred. They flooded the enclosed space with an unearthly scarlet glow and created ominous black shadows.

He peered around the corner and gazed down the flight of stairs.

All clear.

He started down, trying not to clatter. It was difficult to move quickly *and* quietly down the metal stairs.

He turned the corner, gun out in front of him.

No one there.

He darted down the next flight of stairs. As he neared the bottom, he heard a sound—an electrical buzzing, coming from farther down the stairwell. He reached the next landing and paused, listening intently.

No doubt about it. The buzz, louder now, was right around the corner. Mulder took a deep breath, smelling the air in the narrow shaft. That whiff brought back a memory of the train set he'd had as a kid. It was the smell of electricity.

Mulder tensed and tightened his grip on his gun. He spun around the corner, gun leveled, ready to fire at anything that moved.

But the only thing he saw was the steel cover of the sabotaged circuit breaker, gently swinging back and forth on a twisted hinge. The box had been ripped open, and inside bare wires sparked and sizzled, shorting themselves out.

Mulder lowered his gun, his mouth twisted in a grimace of disappointment. Oswald had been here, Mulder knew, but he had no idea where he was now.

Darin stalked through the dark corridors of Connerville Community Hospital. Deep down some part of him knew that he had left the better part of his sanity somewhere far away, but he didn't want to think about that. There was only one thought filling his mind now. One image.

Mrs. Kiveat. Sharon.

Adrenaline coursed through his veins, making him hyperalert. Hyperaware. He could feel his electrical aura expanding around him, like a sixth sense. He could feel the copper wires through the walls, and he could sense heartbeats and brain patterns in the rooms around him. He let that sense of his own power cocoon him against any fear as he strode toward Frank Kiveat's hospital room.

He opened the door and pulled back the curtain. Nothing there. Not even the bed.

"Mrs. Kiveat?"

And then, behind him, he heard a voice. "Darin . . . don't move."

Darin turned. There in the shadows stood Agent Scully, her gun trained on his chest.

He took a long look at the gun and knew he should be frightened. But there was no room in him for fear anymore.

And then out of the darkness behind Scully stepped Sharon Kiveat.

Suddenly the FBI agent and her gun seemed unimportant. He reached out his hand.

"Come with me, Mrs. Kiveat," he said. "There's stuff I need to tell you."

"I want you to step back, Darin," said Scully, the barrel of her gun locked in position.

"Mrs. Kiveat and I are gonna have a talk. Aren't we, Mrs. Kiveat?" Darin kept his hand out, wishing he could use his power to draw her to him.

"Whatever you have to tell her," said Scully, "you can say it right here."

Darin looked into Mrs. Kiveat's eyes. It was too dark to see anything there. "Are you coming?" he asked tenderly.

"She's not going anywhere with you, Darin."

Finally Darin turned his eyes to Scully. She was a perfect target at this close range. He could waste her with a single thought, right then and there.

"I can hurt you!" Darin screamed.

"I can hurt you, too," Scully said, her voice as flat as death. "I'll give you three seconds. One . . ."

"I'm done foolin' around now!" screamed Darin. *"I don't want to fry no FBI agent, but I swear I will."*

"Two!"

And then, like an angel of mercy, Mrs. Kiveat stepped between them. She came to him, just as he'd known she would.

"Stop it!" she shouted at Scully.

Scully pulled back her gun and took a step away. Then Mrs. Kiveat turned to Darin. He could see her eyes now. They were teary. Just like his. *She finally understands,* he thought. *She finally knows how much she means to me.*

And then she said the words he'd been waiting so many months to hear. "I'll go with you, okay?" she said. "I'll go wherever you want. Just don't hurt anyone else."

"I won't hurt nobody," said Darin. "I'll be however you want me to be. Okay, Mrs. Kiveat?"

It was the most wonderful moment of Darin's life.

But then Scully had to ruin it. "We can work everything out right here," she said.

Mrs. Kiveat shook her head. "No, we can't."

Darin took her hand, holding it tightly. Her hand flinched from the slight static shock. Darin smiled, blushing like a little kid.

"All right, then," he said, never taking his eyes off her. "All right."

He put his arm around her waist and backed out of the room, making sure he kept her between himself and Scully's gun. As they left the room, he pulled the door closed. And sent a pulse from his mind that melted the metal of the doorjamb, sealing Scully inside the room.

Chapter FIFTEEN

The chilly air of the parking lot smelled fresh and clean. It smelled like freedom. Suddenly this dark night seemed filled with a kind of light Darin had never known in his life. The light came from Mrs. Kiveat. He could feel her pounding heartbeat as they walked hand in hand. He could sense the wild dancing of her brain waves.

She loves me, he thought.

"You're the only one who was ever nice to me," he told her in a voice warmer and more tender than he'd thought he was capable of. The anger was gone. The people he had hurt, and killed—all that was behind him now. He didn't have to think about them ever again.

"Remember that first day in class?" he asked, still blushing. "You were wearing that green dress, the one with the yellow flowers. You were so pretty." And then he giggled. "I knew right then and there we were meant to be together."

Darin could feel her hand trembling. *Must be from the cold,* he thought.

"Where are we going?" Sharon asked weakly. "Where are you taking me?"

And for the first time, Darin realized that he'd never thought beyond this moment. *Getting* her had always been his goal. But what would he do now that he had her?

"I don't know," he said. "Wherever you want to go, I guess. I got money from the cash machine. And we can take any car you want."

A line of cars stretched out before them. "Just pick one out. An Accord . . . a Maxima . . ." He turned to her. "You like any of those?"

But she didn't seem too happy. He let go of her hand and strolled down the aisle.

"If you don't want to go Japanese, how about a Taurus?" He pushed life into the Ford's ignition. The engine came on, the car's headlights shining across the wet pavement. He shook his head. None of these was good enough for Mrs. Kiveat. She deserved a Mercedes—or better yet, a Ferrari.

"These all stink," he said. "Let's just take one now, and trade it later for something better."

Suddenly, a new set of headlights swept over them. Darin turned and saw a car coming to a stop. It was a police car. Sheriff Teller stepped out of the front seat.

It was just a small problem for Darin—a minor inconvenience. He could deal with Teller.

"Just take it easy now, Mrs. Kiveat," Darin said. "I'll handle this."

He turned to her, but she was no longer there. She was about a hundred yards away, racing from the parking lot into the grassy field beyond it.

"No!" he screamed. But all he could do was watch as the object of his joy and dreams ran away. Once again he was alone—hopelessly alone.

"Hey! You come over here, now!"

Sheriff Teller spoke to Darin Oswald the way he might speak to a rabid dog. And like a wild animal, Darin turned and bolted. Far ahead of them, Sharon Kiveat ducked into a dense grove of trees. She didn't know where she could run, but as long as she stayed out of Darin's sight, she'd stay alive. The night was dark and misty, and although she knew Darin was somewhere close, she thought perhaps he had lost sight of her.

That was when the figure jumped out of the bushes and grabbed her. She tried to scream, but a heavy hand covered her mouth, and she was dragged down into the bushes.

She looked up at her assailant, certain she

would see the burning eyes of Darin Oswald. But instead she saw Agent Mulder.

"Shhh," whispered Mulder. "He's right there."

Together they crouched in the shadows of the bushes, watching as Darin stepped into the grassy clearing.

"Mrs. Kiveat," he pleaded. "Mrs. Kiveat! Where are you?" And then they heard him begin to sob, "Aw, come on now, I said I'd take care of you." He stood there crying like a little boy. But Sharon Kiveat wouldn't step in to comfort him anymore. The depth of the boy's sorrow was matched only by the murderous anger it hid. If Darin saw either of them there in the bushes, they would be incinerated in a matter of seconds.

"What else did you want, Mrs. Kiveat?" he cried to the darkness. "I would have given you anything! Anything you wanted!" Sobs overcame his words.

Then the dim shaft of a single flashlight sliced through the mist.

"Okay, son, turn around," said a commanding voice.

Sheriff Teller faced the boy. "Look, I don't know what kind of trouble you're up to, but I want some answers."

"No! *I* want some answers!" Darin screamed. "Where is she?" A wind swooped down from the treetops and spun around them. *"Come on, now, you're making me mad!"* The clouds above, dark and dense, flashed with immense electrical power. *"Tell me where she is!"*

Mulder came up behind Darin and trained his gun on the boy. "Teller! Get out of there!" he yelled. But Teller was slow to listen to anyone's orders but his own.

"Tell me where she is!" Darin's howl seemed to fill the air, coming from all directions at once. He clenched his fists in rage, and his eyes rolled to the back of his head. A nearby tree exploded with the force of his mind. Sheriff Teller's flashlight blew up in his hand like a grenade and at the same time a pulse of electricity detonated his heart.

Scully made it out of the hospital just in time to see Teller fall to the ground, the damp grass sizzling from the power still shooting through his body.

She and Mulder, their guns drawn, watched in horrified awe as Darin screamed his fury to the skies. Then the heavens answered with a deluge of lightning such as no one had ever seen. White hot and a yard wide, the lightning impaled the berserk Darin Oswald, over and over again, until his shoes had melted; until the grass had burst into flames; until every last fuse blew in his mind and every last light went dark in the cold, lonely town of Connerville.

Chapter SIXTEEN

Fox Mulder stood in the wide corridor of Oklahoma State Psychiatric Hospital. He stared through the pane of unbreakable glass in the door of Darin Oswald's cell. Oswald was sitting inside the small room, facing a nearby TV. The boy's face was blank, his eyes unmoving. It would have been easy to believe that Darin wasn't really seeing anything and that his mind had been wiped clean by that last lightning strike. But Mulder wasn't buying the catatonic act.

The bolt that had knocked Darin down should have killed him. It would have killed half a dozen men. But Darin had awakened a few hours later as if nothing had happened. After a brief period of observation in the emergency ward of Connerville Community Hospital, he had been transferred here. Mulder and Scully had not yet been allowed to question him. Now, two days after the transfer, Mulder was beginning to get the distinct impression that they were never going to have that chance.

Mulder had paid another visit to the Astadourian

Lightning Observatory in Connerville the day before. Once again the scientists there had been maddeningly vague about the work they were doing. Darin's doctor at the psychiatric hospital, who had been so open and frank the first time they spoke, now seemed guarded and suspicious. And just this morning, Mulder and Scully had been ordered back to Washington.

Mulder had seen these signs before.

On their way to the airport, Mulder persuaded Scully that they had time before their flight to stop and try to question Oswald one last time. But Darin's doctor, who was "too busy" to speak to them, sent word that the boy was not to be disturbed.

Mulder heard footsteps. He turned from the cell window to see Scully walking down the corridor toward him.

"I just got off the phone with the coroner," she said. "He's ruling Teller's death accidental."

"Lightning?"

Scully nodded. As if he had to ask.

"And I talked to the D.A.," she went on. "He has no idea how to begin building a case."

Mulder could feel the lid closing on this case despite their best efforts to keep it open. "What about the tests I asked for?" he asked.

"The results just came in." She paused.

"And?"

Scully looked at Mulder with an expression of such tenderness and sympathy that he had to look away. He already knew what that look meant.

"Nothing unusual was detected, Mulder. The electrolytes, the blood gas levels, brain wave activity—"

"All normal." Mulder's voice was flat.

"Yes." Scully nodded. "Based on the data, the scientific evidence . . ." Her voice trailed off.

Mulder took another look through the window at the deranged boy in the cell. "So, according to the 'experts,' Darin Oswald is a perfectly healthy, perfectly normal kid."

Mulder considered Oswald—small, angry, and alone. Abruptly Mulder swung around to stare at his partner. He had one more question to ask her. Suddenly, to him, it was the most important question of all. He had to know. "Scully . . . do *you* believe that?"

Scully looked at her partner.

Mulder took in her silence and knew that she didn't believe it either.

In his padded cell, on the other side of the glass, Darin Peter Oswald gave himself over to the television, changing the channel with his mind again and again. Finally he stopped at the weather channel. A soothing pattern of thin clouds swirled to the north and south, but the weatherman predicted clear skies in the Midwest.

He could sense Scully and Mulder on the other side of the one-way glass. But that didn't matter. They couldn't hurt him. He was important; he was special.

Like Mrs. Kiveat always told him in class, "You young people are the light of the world."

And Darin knew it would soon be his time to shine. No matter what the weatherman said.